To Chuck, my favorite punster in the world
— Cathy

This book is dedicated to the wonderful team that brought Chip and Curly to life.
—Joshua

Sleeping Bear Press™
2395 South Huron Parkway, Suite 200, Ann Arbor, MI 48104
www.sleepingbearpress.com
© Sleeping Bear Press

Printed and bound in the United States.

10 9 8 7 6 5 4 3 2 1

Library of Congress Cataloging-in-Publication Data
Names: Breisacher, Cathy, author. | Heinsz, Joshua, illustrator.
Title: Chip and Curly / written by Cathy Breisacher ; illustrated by Joshua Heinsz.
Description: Ann Arbor, MI : Sleeping Bear Press, [2019] | Summary: Chip the
potato chip is determined to win Spud City's annual sack race, but when
Curly springs into town, Chip worries that his dreams will be mashed.
Identifiers: LCCN 2018037507 | ISBN 9781585364084 (hardcover)
Subjects: | CYAC: Sportsmanship–Fiction. | Competition
(Psychology)–Fiction. | Potatoes–Fiction. | Humorous stories.
Classification: LCC PZ7.B7487 Ch 2019 | DDC [E]–dc23
LC record available at https://lccn.loc.gov/2018037507

Chip and Curly

The Great Potato Race

By Cathy Breisacher

and Illustrated by Joshua Heinsz

PUBLISHED BY SLEEPING BEAR PRESS

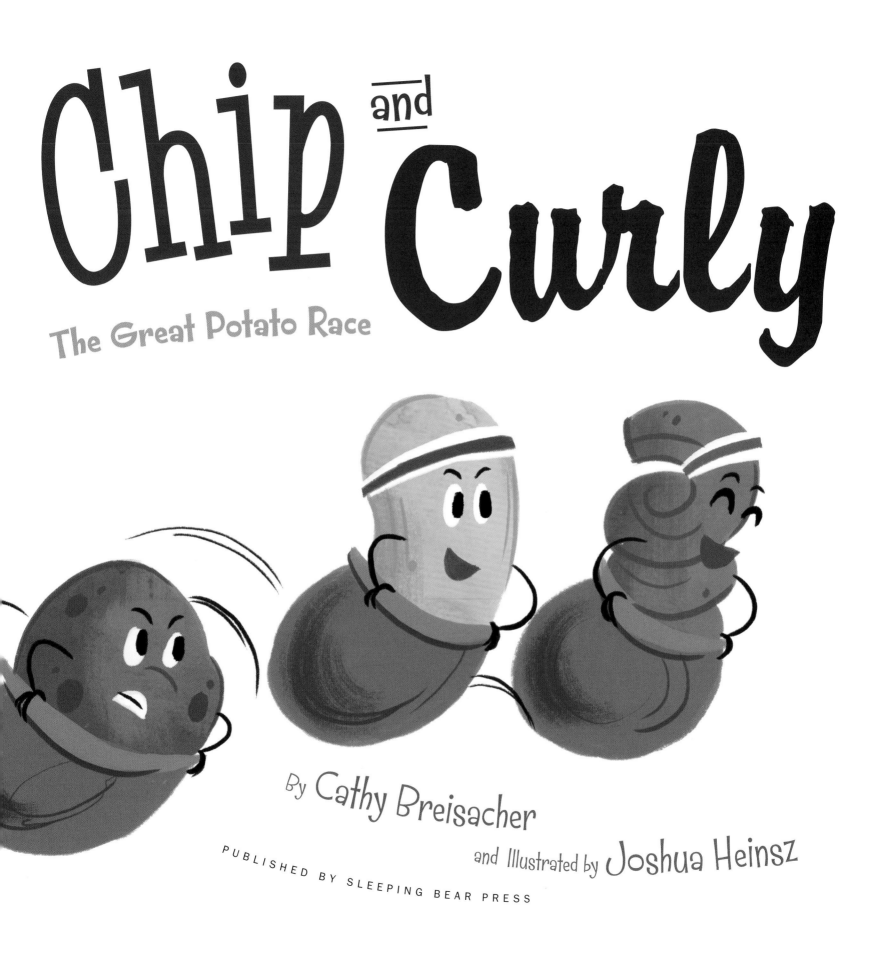

The **Spud City Festival** was just days away and the whole town was getting ready.

Chip's favorite event was the **sack race**, but each year he came up short.

This year he was determined to win the first-place prize: a Golden Bushel Award.

But there was a problem. A new spud had arrived in town.

Curly. And he had quite a spring in his step.

"He's fast," Chip thought.

So he practiced every chance he got.

"There's our guy!" the Roasted Yams boasted as Chip leapt by.

"You're our **hometown favorite,**" hollered the Home Fries.

Still, Chip felt nervous.

The morning of the festival, Chip arrived early to study the race path.

Meanwhile, the crowd gathered.

The Couch Potatoes lined the race route.

The French Fries stood with their Tater Tots.

And the Sweet Potatoes practiced cheers.

After stretching, Chip high-fived the Tots and posed for pictures.

Everything was going great until ...

Curly arrived, leaping toward
the other racers. Chip groaned.

To top it off, Curly wedged in next
to him at the starting line.

Chip gripped his sack and stared straight ahead.
He wanted to win more than ever.

"Ready! Set! Go!" said the announcer. The potatoes hopped forward, and Chip **whipped** past everyone.

"CHIP! CHIP! CHIP!" chanted the crowd.

"I've got this in the bag," he thought.

"Keep moving! Keep moving!" the Twice Bakes repeated.

Chip heard someone gaining on him—but he didn't look back.

"Look out!" the BBQ Chips shouted. **"Here comes a hot potato!"**

And then it happened.
Curly pulled ahead.
The crowd went wild.

Even the Couch Potatoes stood up and took notice.

The Waffle Fries couldn't decide who to cheer for.

Chip hopped faster, but he couldn't catch up. Just ahead, a tree root stuck out of the ground. Chip had his eye on it. But Curly headed right toward it.

Curly tripped and tumbled to the ground.
A thought sprouted in Chip's mind ...
with Curly down, this was his chance to win.
He zipped past Curly and took the lead.

OOMPH!!

But as the finish line came
into view, he felt rotten.
Chip glanced over his shoulder.
He hashed it over in his mind.

FINISH!

There was only one thing to do. He bounded toward Curly, who lay pancaked on the ground.

Chip reached down and pulled him up while the other potatoes bounced by.

"One potato,
two potato,
three potato, four,"
counted the announcer as the racers
entered the final stretch of the course.
"Five potato, six potato,
seven potato—wait!
Here come two more!"

Curly and Chip had hopped back
onto the path and were picking up speed.

In a flash, Curly peeled ahead of the pack with Chip on his heels.
As they neared the end of the race,
Chip barreled along and gave it all he had.

But it was no use.
Curly sprang across the finish line.
In an instant, Chip's dreams of winning were mashed.

The Sweet Potatoes cheered.
The other racers congratulated Curly.

"They're going to butter him up now,"
Chip muttered.

He slipped out of his sack and
tossed it onto a pile.

As he turned to leave, Curly stopped him.
"The relay is next. Want to be my partner?"

Chip froze in his steps. "Me?"

"Sure! No matter how you slice it,
we'd make a great team."

A smile sprouted on Chip's face.
"Okay, Bud, let's do it."

They practiced on the sidelines.

Before long, they were in a groove.

"Maybe I'll finally win a Golden Bushel Award," said Chip.

But there was a problem.

A new team had arrived.

The Shoestring Fries.
They were lean and snappy,
and moved in perfect step.